# The Bird on the Wire

## ...and other stories

Edited by

Bobby Cadwallader

**Cadwallader**
**Aylesbury, Buckinghamshire**

Cadwallader
ISBN: 978-1-3999-4671-1

## Acknowledgements:

We would like to thank Alan Corkish for his unstinting support, plentiful advice, steadfast encouragement and his speed. Without his generous assistance in putting our anthology together our project would never have been completed.

# Dedication

This book is dedicated to Jackie Rickard, a much-loved friend, wife, mother and grandmother whose contribution to the Aylesbury U3A is missed by the many who met her. Her writing, included in this anthology, reflects our memories of her personality and warmth. Jackie died suddenly in June 2022 aged 74. We miss her so much.

# Contents

Contents

## Foreword

Our group has been together for about five years and we enjoy sharing our work at our monthly meetings. During lockdown we continued to send our pieces to each other and later on we met over zoom to read our work aloud again. Although we have a theme each month, we are constantly amazed by how different our ideas and approaches are.

We have put this anthology together after each choosing five favourite pieces of our own work and then ranking each other's choices in order to select four from each writer. Even this process caused some surprises.

So here we present you an eclectic bunch of stories written over several years. We hope you have as much pleasure reading them as we did writing and sharing them.

# The Bird on the Wire
Bob Close

I'm an early riser and the beginning of my day is nearly always the same.

Shortly after waking I will go down to the kitchen, half fill the electric kettle and switch it on. As it begins to heat up, I go into the living room and switch on the TV. Going back to the kitchen I make a cup of tea then return to the living room. I sip at the tea as I watch the morning news items or check the first emails of the day on my laptop. By the time I have finished my tea all is well with the world even if, according to the news, the world is anything but well.

Aah the power of ritual, with a little help from caffeine. So, it was on one bright June morning at our home in the market town of Bridport in 2012. What made this day a little special was the presence of our friends, Ivan and Peachy, from Australia. They were staying with us for a couple of days as part of a two-month tour of Europe and had arrived the night before.

Tea drunk, world well, I went to the kitchen sink to wash the tea cup. As I did so I gazed out at our back garden and spotted a fuzzy but bright, red and blue shape, perhaps a trapped balloon or a piece of cellophane, on the wire connecting telegraph pole to house. Believe it or not my eyesight, or at least my long vision, has improved since then but at that time, to make out the intriguing spectre, I required my glasses. Once located (a long short story in itself) I put them on, focused on the fuzz and resolved the shape. It was not, as I had thought, a balloon; it was a bird. And what a bird it was!

The bird on the wire had a bright red body with blue wings and tail. The colours were intense and vibrant and my strong suspicion was that this was not an indigenous species. 'Proper little Sherlock Holmes' you will say and you will be even less impressed when I tell you that my deduction was strengthened by the clearly parrot like beak on the aforementioned avian. This, I thought to myself, *is* a parrot but then its lack of movement raised in my mind the possibility that it was not a *real* parrot. Perhaps it was a toy or model which had by some mysterious means been carried up by a gust of wind and snared itself on the telephonic conduit. Either that or it was displaying all the tell-tale signs of the Monty Python Norwegian Blue; to whit, it was a dead parrot.

I was idly ruminating on the latter when the bird, perhaps telepathic and offended, turned its head and looked directly at me. The look was of a penetrating and malevolent intensity that I have never experienced from a parrot either before or since. From my dear wife, Mary, yes; but not a parrot. Then, to further communicate that offence had been taken, Pretty Polly ruffled her feathers and shuffled sideways along the wire. Norwegian Blue! How dare you!

'A Rosella' said a voice beside me. It was our guest Ivan, another early riser. 'Didn't know you had parrots in England'.

'We don't' I said. 'What did you say it was?'

'A Rosella, a Rosella parakeet. Pretty bird, lots of them back home in Australia. How did that one get here?'

I gazed at him deadpan.

'Well, we thought you might be homesick so I bought one yesterday and stuck him in the garden so you would feel more at home in the morning'.

Ivan looked puzzled, was about to respond and then smiled. 'Yeah, yeah, come on Bob how did it get here?'

'Perhaps you or Peachy brought it with you for similar 'feeling at home' reasons.' I said.

Ivan laughed but I suspected that he was tempted to ask Peachy what exactly it was that she had brought over in that very large suitcase.

Eventually having established that neither of us or our partners had released said parrot into the garden we agreed that it must be an escapee and therefore we should endeavour to capture this rapture in red and blue and return it to its rightful owner. But who was the owner and how would we entrap this 'beaut' of a bird, as Ivan might say? (He didn't, since he was not a stereotypical 'Aussie', or Australian, as he would put it.). First things first, so we wisely, or so we thought, decided to devise a hunting strategy.

They say that necessity is the mother of invention and so it was that thirty minutes later we emerged into the garden (or 'outback' as Ivan might have said, but as you have predicted, didn't) with a child's fishing net, one packet of Honey Roast Salted Peanuts and a bowl of red lentils. Ivan laid a trail of nuts and lentils and I waited, net raised, cunningly concealed at the back of the garden shed. The Rosella, clearly a fussy breakfast eater, took one look at the nut and lentil buffet and flew off to another garden in search of better fare.... perhaps a 'Full English', who knows? By this time other neighbours had been alerted and 'The Great Bridport Parrot Hunt' was in full flow. Many and varied were the parrot traps devised, involving bananas, bread, banana bread, sticky toffee pudding, sticks, buckets, bed-knobs, broomsticks and much besides, but to no avail. At the end of the morning this bird had flown.

Exhausted hunters and hunt followers convened, not 'under the shade of a coolabah tree', as Ivan might have said (he didn't), but in our kitchen, sharing tea and biscuits and our thoughts on the remarkable co-incidence that had united (or was it re-united?), itinerant Australian tourists with an apparently migratory Australian parrot.

Some mysteries may never be solved.

But wait.

Later that day a local radio station reported that a bird fancier in Weymouth, only sixteen miles from Bridport, had asked listeners to look out for an escaped parrot. We phoned the station.

It was not that parrot.

And then.

This bloke round the corner told a mutual acquaintance, who told me, that one of his parrots had escaped while he was cleaning out his aviary.

It came back two days later.

That's the one.

~~~~

# Christmas
## Christine Campbell

Last Christmas was a bit of a blur to me. My partner of seven years, Simon, died early in November from a brain tumour that we had no knowledge of until spring that year. We had hardly begun the round of hospital appointments, chemo and radiotherapy treatments before I found myself visiting not a hospital but a hospice and by Thanksgiving I was back in the arms of my large, loving family, no longer the independent city girl but a red-eyed, wild-haired throwback to my teenage years, looking out from the window of my childhood bedroom on the Cape across the cranberry bogs to the ocean, hoping and praying that I would see Simon returning from an extended fishing trip, smiling and waving.

My family scooped me up and hid me from the world. I returned to our apartment in Boston for a few days before Christmas, during which time I made a feeble attempt to fit back into the world of my co-workers, some who had obviously read the office guidelines for what to say to a bereaved colleague, and others who decided it was better not to refer to the unfortunate episode at all. But there were others, like Matilda, maybe because they were older and had more experience of these things, took time to ask how I was and call Simon by name when speaking of those last unbearable months.

Matilda invited me to her church on the Sunday before Christmas, before I returned to the Cape for the holidays. I was dubious, having only attended churches for the weddings of my siblings and that was more for show than any deep religious conviction on their or my part. However, what struck me on visiting Matilda's church was how friendly and welcoming everyone was. After the service they gathered together for coffee and home-made cake and once a month, put on a lunch that was remarkable given the confines of the kitchen and average age of the helpers. It was the church's mission to help the local homeless population, mainly men who wandered in towards the end of the service carrying their lives in black garbage bags or rucksacks which they would leave by the door, then make themselves as inconspicuous as possible at tables where kindly church members made sure they could be included in the conversation; a task that I initially found uncomfortable and difficult as I'm sure they must have.

So, as I say last Christmas at home was a blur. Each year our family takes it in turns to host, having three older sisters and a brother, all married with children. It's a joyful, noisy haphazard affair and I was able to lose myself in the chaos of children opening presents, dogs running amok among the debris of wrapping paper and being given a hasty domestic chore every time I looked like I was going to collapse in a weeping mass.

Despite my mother being a single parent to us all since my father left when I was seven, Christmases were always special. Being the youngest I barely noticed the difference my father leaving meant. My sisters and brother were teenagers, and although I didn't realise it at the time, they felt a great sense of relief. I hadn't been so affected by our father's drink fuelled rants and threats to our mother but looking back I think something of the relief also rubbed off on me and none of us cared that we never heard from him again. Later my mother remarried to a schooldays sweetheart who had returned to the town when his wife died. Bob neatly filled the father-shaped gap in my life, and it was he who walked my sisters down the aisle on their wedding days.

Strangely enough the one thing I remember about my father at Christmas was a silly phrase he used to say when we sat down to eat: "God bless this Christmas dinner and God knows how I'm going to eat it all!". I still used to think of it at later Christmas meals, but even as a child knew to keep the thought to myself.

This year at Thanksgiving, spent at my middle sister's house, I managed to conduct myself well enough without breaking down, and announced then that Christmas this year being on a Tuesday, I would visit over the preceding weekend then return to Boston on Christmas Eve. Matilda had invited me to her house that evening and I planned to help out at the Christmas Day lunch the church organised for the homeless community; now I was a dab hand at rustling up meals in the cramped kitchen and hopefully accomplished at making our guests feel at ease.

This of course was met with alarm by my family that I shouldn't be alone, it was still early days and we're always together at Christmas. But I stood my ground, although it would have been so easy to say, 'Well ok then' and revert to cosseted teenager in my sister's spare bedroom.

I returned to a magical scene straight out of a Christmas movie with a light dusting of snow on the sidewalks and the reflection of lights all along the Charles River. The Christmas Eve service did make me cry but I now had some belief that things would get better and I could move on with my life.

Resplendent in snowflake sweater, Santa hat and jingle bell earrings, I waited behind the red and green festooned table ready to add the final touch of gravy to the heaving plates of turkey and all the trimmings being proffered by the remarkably spruced up homeless guests.

Finally sitting down amongst them to enjoy my meal, my eye is caught by an elderly white-haired man at the end of the table. There's something familiar about him and as he goes to take his first mouthful, he pauses and says to no one in particular, "God bless this Christmas dinner and God knows how I'm going to eat it all!".

~~~

# She's my best friend... I hate her...
## Bobby Cadwallader

Susie and Eloise had been friends from the cradle. Born within a few hours of each other, to best friend mothers, they knocked bricks down together at day care, fought over the trikes at preschool and learned to read in the same week in kindergarten. They even gained their yellow belts in karate on the same day. In the elementary grades they enjoyed giggling sleepovers and making up tall stories to frighten each other; learning to braid each other's hair and sharing secrets. As they progressed to middle school, they followed the same pursuits and hobbies and they both graduated from high school with the same good grades.

Then overnight everything changed. An amateur opera group came to Almaden Valley. The young directors were looking for a lead for Carmen. Both girls were keen singers, performing enthusiastically in the school choir and singing in chapel on Sundays. Their eagle eyes both alighted on the advert in the Lake Park as they strolled home from school on a scorching afternoon in May at the end of their final year. Auditions were to take place in the Community Centre the week after school was out. In unison they exclaimed, "I'd like to play Carmen." Then they each looked at the other guiltily as if they wished they'd bitten their lips. For the first time in their closely entwined lives the girls did not discuss this further and neither divulged to the other that she was practising in private.

The day of the auditions dawned hot and sunny. There was no breeze as the two girls walked down through the park to the Community Centre in silence. They strolled with no acrimony, but with each secretly not wanting success for the other; an alien feeling for both of them. This was a first. They had always championed each other. They had never been rivals. The afternoon was long and stressful. At the end of each tense round eliminations took place. By 6pm, incredibly, only Eloise and Susie were left. "It's a tough decision girl, but I am going to have to choose Eloise. She has the stronger and, indeed, finer voice, and her dark hair is just so right for Carmen. Of course, Susie, we would like you to understudy the part, as well as joining the chorus. Is that OK?"

Choking back the tears Susie nodded her assent, but she was unable to congratulate her best friend or even acknowledge her success. They walked home, as they had arrived, in deathly silence. This time however there was a palpable tension in the air: their steaming moods reflecting the end of this pressure cooker day.

Rehearsals did not start until the following week. In those long drawn out seven days Susie neither rang nor called for her friend. After one abortive call from Eloise with Susie pleading a sickness bug Eloise diplomatically decided to leave her friend alone for a while. Rehearsals began with a vengeance. Every night for a month they were expected to sing, act and dance for three hours. In normal circumstances it would have been tough but for Susie it was utter torture to watch her friend blossoming and receiving the plaudits that she would have loved herself, not to mention that gorgeous Spanish tiered dress which was being made especially to fit her friend's slim body. Her sense of duty would not allow her to renege on her agreement but she found it almost impossible. Each morning she woke with a heavy weight in her stomach and by the end of each day her jealousy had driven her ever further inside herself. She neither slept nor ate well, so all-consuming was her envy.

On the Saturday before the show, she got up at 5.30am with an aching head from lack of sleep and took herself off for a walk around Almaden Lake to try to clear her head and to make some sense of her emotions. Her hope that the sparkling water and gentle croaking of the frogs would soothe her turmoil were in vain. She arrived home to a spookily quiet house. There was a note on the table from her mum summoning her to Eloise's house. Fearing some kind of showdown, she was reluctant to go. Her resentment rose like bile to the surface again. It was so bitter she could taste it. Why should she be the one to climb down? She donned her bike helmet and pedalled the three blocks over a route so familiar she could have done it blindfold. She was taken aback to see a police car parked outside.

"Susie thank goodness. We had no idea where you were," exclaimed her mum. Susie looked over her mum's shoulder to where Eloise's mum sat, looking shrunken and small; her eyes red rimmed.

Susie's heart skipped a beat. "What's happened? Is Eloise OK? She's not dead, is she?"

"No darling but she's had a very nasty accident. She is in hospital with a broken leg and several broken ribs. Nevertheless, she is asking for you. Crying because of your quarrel. Her heart is breaking. Nothing will console her. She needs you."

Thirty minutes later Susie sat at her friend's bedside holding her hand and declaring, "I am so sorry. It is all my fault."

"Don't be daft," replied Eloise kindly, "you weren't driving the truck. Still, you will have to play Carmen now."

Susie's face fell. Nothing had been further from her thoughts. All she cared about was that Eloise was safe. "I can't." she wailed. "It's your part."

"You must," said Eloise" you absolutely must do it for me; for us, for our friendship. You will be brilliant."

A week later Susie sang to a packed house. She brought the house down with a beautiful rendition of 'Love is a rebellious bird'; she received a standing ovation and four curtain calls. However, it was not the leading lady who received the huge bouquet of flowers. It was the girl on the front row with the crutches. The note read,

"With all my love to Eloise. Best friends forever: rivals never."

~~~

# The Passengers
## Hazel Burgess

The Passenger Terminal at Heathrow was heaving with people anxious to get away. Andreas strode through the Departure Lounge purposefully. Today was to be the day. As Co-Pilot he was going to show what he was made of. How dare anybody say that he was unfit to fly?

He passed an elderly couple fussing with a wheelchair, carrying the frail gentleman. He assumed it was his wife, flapping around him and mopping the drool from his chin. Rushing on, Andreas was determined that he would never end up like that.

Close by, an attractive Asian teenager scanned the passengers entering the lounge. Yasmin was watching out for another girl, Safia. She clutched the handle of her small black wheelie, containing just enough for a couple of nights in Switzerland, and a small backpack to use when she arrived. The problem was, she did not know what Safia looked like, only that she would be wearing a union jack t-shirt. That seemed very ironic to Yasmin, but she had dutifully left her hijab behind. Her father would be very angry but his domination was the very reason why she was flying to Switzerland. At sixteen, she now felt very grown up. How mortifying it had been when her father would not let her have a party, with boys, to celebrate her recent birthday. She would show him! Nervously, she took a small mirror out of her pocket, examining her makeup. Unused to wearing western cosmetics, she felt conspicuous, even amongst the anonymous crowds. Her father thought she was staying with a school friend, for a shopping trip. The flower in her button-hole drooping, she anxiously tried to protect the velvety petals, just as she was tapped on the shoulder. Caught already – no, she espied the British flag. Now the adventure would begin.

The distinguished, grey-haired gentleman sitting next to Monica helped her push the wheelchair when the flight was called. She assumed he was a businessman, probably in banking, heading to a meeting. She thought of the paperwork in her bag – it had a finality about it. Hubert had been determined to go and Switzerland had seemed extra fitting, given the wonderful walking holidays they had had there in their youth, when he was able to walk, and talk, properly. Smiling nostalgically, she remembered their honeymoon – no plane then but a hard, long, monotonous boat and train journey right through to the Alps. There they had started their married life together, where, soon, it would all end. How would she manage without her rock and lifelong partner?

By her side, Bill felt the uncomfortable package sitting in his groin. He had nearly made it. Never in a million years had he thought that he would be consorting with the criminal fraternity again, at seventy- five. Alright, he had only played a small part in the heist, but he had his reward and was fleeing with it. Of course, it had been a major crime, filling the headlines for days and only an hour ago he had read the billboards which proclaimed the raid and searching of his colleagues' homes. What luck, that he could camouflage himself escorting this old pair.

Sitting on the plane Yasmin showed Safia her phone. She had deleted all photos which showed her family in eastern dress – the pictures of her sister's wedding in Pakistan, her mother at home and her father ready to attend the mosque last Friday. Now she had nothing to remember them by. Swallowing the sudden tears, she started to think of the new husband awaiting her. What would he look like? She imagined his strong physique, masculine, bearded face and brown skin – like a Bollywood movie star. After all, as a fighter, he was bound to be what her school friends would term to be a 'hunk'. Safia nodded. Once they landed, they would go to a named guesthouse and from there book the next, but not final, leg of the journey – another plane to Istanbul. They would then travel very light on the coach taking them to the border, where they would meet a guide to take them into Syria. She would not have to hide her faith there.

Across the aisle, Monica looked at her sleeping husband and fingered the instructions in her pocket. They were to be met by an ambulance, with escort. This had cost their life savings. Dignitas – the name had a comforting ring about it. All Hubert wanted was his dignity back – some quality of life. That was not to be, so she had agreed to let him go. Oh yes, he had left a letter saying it was his wish and nothing to do with her. He had tried to show her what to do on her return, to ensure she could continue to live comfortably – stocks, shares, valuables held in a safety deposit box, although there was no money left in the bank, until the next pension instalment went in. Mind wandering, she espied the headline of the paper held by the man in front – pity those people who had lost all their valuables in the recent robbery in Hatton Gardens.

Sitting next to the same man, Bill's insides turned to water. He had been 'straight' for over twenty years. Why had he let his ego be so flattered that he had agreed to help his old mate and son when they told him about the planned crime of the decade – it would see him living in comfort for the rest of his life they promised? However, would exile be the way he wanted to end his days? He stiffened in shock as he saw the uniformed guy coming his way, only to let out a sigh of relief when he realised it was the captain going to the toilet. They would be landing shortly – he would stick by the elderly couple through customs and then find somewhere to stay, incognito.

The commotion startled the passengers. Hubert opened his eyes as the captain started to bang on the cockpit door, shouting, "For Christ's sake, open this door." Yasmin dropped her phone; Monica felt the instructions flutter to the floor. Bill closed his eyes and started to pray, asking for forgiveness of his sins.

The plane, piloted by Andreas, started its sudden, unexpected descent, quickly heading for the highest peaks in the mountain range. Then oblivion...

~~~

# The Road Trip
Jackie Rickard

Well, here we were fast approaching the end of the Summer Term at School. Reports had been received, scrutinised and duly signed back to the children's teachers and last-minute goodbyes and leaving events attended. We were on our holidays at last!!

La Baule here we come again. The next thing to do was pack our caravan which luckily, we store at the side of the house. Buckets, spades, beach games, lilos, the faithful old, yellow and green pump-up dinghy complete with pump this time and every conceivable swimwear, camping equipment, in fact almost as the saying goes, everything except the kitchen sink.

We had been going to one of our favourite sites in France for many years both on our own as a family or with friends but it didn't matter which group, we went with there were always friendly families to meet up with again and again, year after year. Camping Tremondec was quite a basic campsite with each emplacement surrounded on three sides with hedges, a shop that was more like an Aladdin's cave stocking food, ice creams, wine and the smell always of freshly baked long French sticks of bread. And then there was the site owner, Monsieur Champenois who drove around the site chatting to everyone making sure they were enjoying everything about their holiday. There was never any paperwork involved when you arrived on site, oh yes, we had booked the previous year as we had left ready for the following summer but not really an official type of booking, it just got put down in a rather large blue lined paper folder. When it came to paying the bill Monsieur C. always wrote l'addition in the dust on his old Citroen motor roof and that is how he ran the business, nothing formal just laid back and so friendly.

The caravan hitched safely onto the car, two children counted into the car surrounded by toys, books, snacks and we were off. We always made it a habit to drive round the block a couple of times before actually setting off as there is always something someone has forgotten. One year we forgot to pack the pillows and most importantly of all, favourite teddy, so that drive around the block before actually consulting the map is a necessity if we are to avoid tears or more importantly a quick return trip of anything up to 50 miles!!

Are we there yet? ...no not yet, seems to be the only words spoken for a few miles until we embark on the old favourite of 'I Spy' or even who can see a red car first, then a green one, then a yellow lorry...

Portsmouth to Le Havre is our favourite route across the Channel so a drive to Portsmouth Quayside, park the caravan in a bay with the hitch lock firmly in place and then a quick visit to Dave's favourite Aunty Dorothy who has lived in Portsmouth all her life. Knowing we are 'just calling in' she is a true diamond and always enjoys the company and most importantly making cakes and scones for a quick afternoon tea.

That done and it's back to the Port, hitch the caravan back onto the car and board the 3.00pm sailing for Le Havre. The vehicles are packed so tightly into the decks, we squeeze out of the car doors, up the steps onto the observation's decks just as the last of the cars and vans are boarding, the bow doors are secured and we are away. As we round Sally Port, we wave frantically to Aunty Dorothy who has come down to the quayside to wave us off on our journey firstly making us promise to call in on our return 4 weeks later!!

The sailing takes about 6 hours so we usually watch Portsmouth gradually fade into the distance and then have a bit of a wander around the ship before settling into a comfy seating area near the cafeteria, eat our tea whilst Dave studies the map ready for disembarkation.

It is quite dark when we dock at 9.00pm but the excitement of our holidays and finding the Port exit towards the Tankerville Bridge keeps us all on our toes and nobody is remotely tired. Over the Bridge to an area which is safe and many caravans are parked up for the night ready for the longish drive the next day to the campsite. Beds in the caravan are quickly made up and we all try to snuggle down for a few hours' sleep. Suddenly, crunching of stones under shoes wakes us all up and opening the curtains we soon discover there are very few of us still here whilst most are already on the open road.

The children call out road numbers to our driver whilst I

take in the beautiful countryside full of sunflowers, corn on the cob, apple trees and much more. Soon we spot the Boulangerie and stop off for some fresh bread and cheese that will be our lunch. There are so many pull in areas for travellers with wooden benches and play areas for the children to eat and then stretch their legs running around before the next stage of our journey.

This journey to La Baule, the most beautiful beach area on the Atlantic with smaller seaside towns within easy reach, never seems too long or boring. The excitement of a month in this lovely area has always been a favourite alongside Manuel's!! Manuel's is a double fronted corner shop right on the shoreline of La Baule overlooking the beach. Noses pressed against the glass windows and can be seen toffee, rock, chocolate and indeed all sorts of delights being freshly made. It is a firm favourite for many and a small bag of sweet delights on a balmy evening walking along the sea front is a must especially on Assumption Day, August 15th when the whole town comes alive with bands, street food, entertainers and fabulous fireworks coming out of the sea late at night.

The roads are now getting narrower and more rural, Chateaux seem to be around every bend and we have played out our 'I Spy' alongside the coloured cars and lorries but suddenly around another dusty corner and Camping Tremondec is there in front just as it was last year and the year before, nothing has changed and we have arrived.

Hugs and kisses are the normal greeting and we are soon shown onto our emplacement, the children have happily skipped off to the play area with other children from France, Germany and England whilst we set up the 'van, fill the water tanks, table and chairs out and a nice cold glass of beer compliments of the site owner. It has been a happy and safe road trip; one we have done many times and hopefully will continue to do in the future.

~~~

# New Horizons
## Bob Close

You ask what I remember of that day. I remember it all.

The great storm had passed and our village had been re-built. The easy rhythm of our life had returned.

My father woke me with a gentle shake. "Quiet" he said "the others are still asleep but if we go now, we can be first to the sea grass". I followed him from the hut and we walked down the white beach to our canoe. The sun had not yet risen but it was light and I could see the waves breaking on the reef. As we paddled out over the still waters of the lagoon, I asked my father what was beyond the reef.

"Beyond the Eastern horizon there is nothing, only sea" he said. "But on the other side of this island, to the West, there are many other islands and a land without sea. On that land the Great Mother created our people and from there we ventured East from island to island. Now we are at that journey's end. Here we have found our rightful place, here on Guanahan. Those who have ventured further out to the East have never returned. It is a void. But my son why should we leave this place? It has all we need and more. Sharpen the knives while you sit there: we are nearly at the meadows".

I did what I was told and my father paddled the canoe on towards the reef. Soon beneath us I could make out the long swaying green strands of sea grass.

My father ceased paddling and rested. He would dive first. He began slow steady breaths then on one long final intake of air he fell backwards into the water and descended. I could see him over the grass his hands parting the strands, patiently searching. The rising sun distracted me and I looked out to the East thinking of the endless void that lay there. A splash and gasp interrupted my thoughts as my father surfaced alongside the canoe. He raised his hand triumphantly, in it a large Queen Conch. He threw it into the canoe and smiled at me. "It is a good day" he said and returned to the depths.

With twenty or so conch in the boat it was time to head back to the village. The sun was now making its way across the sky and the village would have come to life. I looked out again at the Eastern horizon as my father began to turn the canoe.

"Stop, stop I shouted, there's something there".

He was not pleased.

"What can be there? The sun has got your eyes, I've told you before don't look at it".

But there *was* something there. As we looked three shapes took form. They seemed to be canoes but larger than I had ever seen and impossibly tall, rising out from the water as if they must fall. But they did not and as they came nearer, we saw men on the vessels, dressed in cloth and shiny metal. Finally, we heard shouts but we could not understand what they were saying. Their vessels could not cross over the reef and we pointed South knowing that they would have access to the shore in crab bay. As they sailed away, we headed back across the lagoon in great excitement to tell the others what we had seen.

Yes, I remember it clearly. That was the day our lives changed, never to return to the way of life the Great mother had given us.

Would that we had never pointed.

That day our misery and ordeal began. You have taken the land we had and now you are removing the last of us from it. "Senor, where will you send us?'

Ah yes, of course, to the mines of Hispaniola.

Twenty years ago, was that day. Three ships came from the void; three ships sailed West to new horizons.

But for us it was the end.

~~~

# Flowers
## Christine Campbell

Charlie bought flowers for Janet every Friday, had done since they started dating back in the sixties. It was on an impulse one Friday night on his way to meet Janet outside the Odeon; he passed by a flower seller outside the station. He had enough to pay for two tickets in the stalls though it might mean he would go without an ice cream in the interval.

Back in those days the man paid for everything and anyway Janet was still at college and only had a Saturday job. He was an apprentice car mechanic and although his wages weren't great, by cycling to work and taking homemade sandwiches he could give his mum half his wages and manage to afford a weekly outing to the cinema with Janet on a Friday night. On Saturday evenings they took it in turns to watch television round each other's houses, squashed up on the sofa with Janet's two younger brothers, or at a discrete distance on his mother's sofa, with his parents in their respective armchairs either side of the fireplace.

Janet was quite overcome when she received that first bunch of daffodils. It was the first time anyone had bought her flowers and it made her feel quite grown up and sophisticated. Her mother, who had never received more than a box of Milk Tray from her father, thought that Charlie was very gallant; not a word that Janet was familiar with, but she did think she had found someone very special with Charlie and hoped they would be together for ever.

As it turned out they were the perfect fit, neither was interested in looking further afield. Charlie became a qualified mechanic and started specialising in classic sports cars, eventually by buying and renovating sufficient cars he was able to open his own garage. Janet passed her secretarial course and worked at a solicitor's office in the town. They saved enough money to put a deposit on a two-bedroom semi-detached house where every Friday Janet would throw away one bunch of flowers and add a fresh one when Charlie walked through the door in the evening.

Over the years the flowers were simple bouquets usually bought from the local supermarket but sometimes, if Charlie had to work late, they were from the garage and not really to Janet's taste. However, she realised how lucky she was and never showed any dissatisfaction.

The years went by. Three children, a boy and two girls, spaced at two yearly intervals, added to the happy household and on the birth of each one a beautiful bouquet was delivered with a card proclaiming Charlie's love and gratitude.

Not long after the birth of Carol, the youngest, the quality of the Friday bouquets began to improve. Janet remarking on this asked if Charlie had gone to a different supermarket. Charlie responded that there was a stall in the layby near his garage so he would probably buy them from there in future. Janet said she hoped they weren't too expensive, but they did look lovely.

One afternoon Janet was going to see an old school friend who had just come out of hospital. The friend lived on the side of town where Charlie had his garage and as it was a Friday, she thought she would stop at the flower stall in the layby. There was only one layby near the garage and apart from the regular snack van it was empty. Janet had no choice but to stop at the petrol station, which didn't sit well with her at all. She hoped her friend would be of the opinion 'it's the thought that counts'.

Later that evening when Charlie produced the usual bunch of flowers Janet asked as casually as she could manage if they had come from the layby seller. Of course, was the reply. Later Janet wondered why she hadn't mentioned her fruitless visit to the layby. The location wasn't in doubt as Charlie often used the snack van. He was quite friendly with the couple who ran it, who when Janet had enquired as to the whereabouts of the flower seller, had looked at each other quizzically and confirmed they were the only people serving the layby; there was not and never had been a flower seller; but something was telling Janet to leave well alone.

Hard strenuous work eventually took its toll on Charlie. One morning he wasn't the first up to make a cup of tea and bring up to Janet still snoozing in bed. As Janet watched the rapid departure of the blue lighted ambulance, she knew life would never be the same.

It was a beautiful spring day when Janet entered the florist.

It had been many years since she had visited such a place due to never needing to buy flowers for herself and if for others, she would call in to the upmarket supermarket she favoured or make a call to Interflora. Today her needs were more specific, and it required all her composure to convey to the pleasant middle-aged assistant what she needed.

Deborah closed the door on the customer and turned the wooden sign to closed; although it was not quite three in the afternoon, she needed some time and was grateful that today she had the shop to herself. What had started as a comforting chat with the recently bereaved woman who tried so hard to keep her tears at bay, had turned Deborah's world upside down. The woman had told her how throughout her 52 years of marriage her husband had bought her flowers every Friday; now it was her turn to buy one last bouquet for him.

Deborah always wondered why Charlie suddenly stopped all contact. Part of their arrangement had been no discussion of their other lives. They both knew each had commitments and lives that they did not want to leave but for a few hours every Friday afternoon the world outside was paused and they existed only for each other.

As Deborah carefully placed the last white rose into the sheaf and tied the dark blue ribbon a tear fell unnoticed from her eye.

Janet hardly took her eyes away from the sheaf of white roses tied with ribbon the colour of Charlie's football team. Later outside, standing where the flowers had been placed, she noticed the card written on her behalf by the florist. It had not been raining and the card was enclosed in a plastic cover but the row of kisses at the end of the message ended in a blur of ink.

~~~

# The Sound of Seagulls
### Bobby Cadwallader

The sound of seagulls always reminded her of that day, albeit was nearly half a century ago. That screeching filled her head with memories of that terrible anxiety, that dreadful two hours she spent searching. The tide rolling in an out in an exciting, but also slightly threatening way adding to her terrors. It had been a glorious summer's day. The kids playing happily on the beach, squealing with delight as the waves chased them up the beach. They were constantly charging up to her to reveal their latest finds of razor shells and interesting pebbles. "I love this one mummy. Can I take it home?" They had enjoyed a picnic on the sands making the usual jokes about sand sandwiches, and Toby spilling his juice in his chaotic four-year-old way. The picnic over, they begged her to let them go exploring in the rock pools. The sun was making her drowsy so she gave in and let them unpack their fishing nets and paddle through the shallows to the rocks just visible on the horizon. She watched amused as they chattered to each other animatedly, and, dragging their nets behind them, they ran joyfully to the inviting pools. As the sun blazed down, she removed her glasses and lay back on the warm sand.

What seemed like five minutes later she woke with a start. Looking towards the rock pools she failed to spy the two children and sat up in a panic. Glancing at her watch she realised she had been asleep for nearly 30 minutes. Horrified she rushed over to the pools calling out their names. "Toby, Susie where are you? We need to pack up." As she approached the glistening little ponds, she realised with horror that they were not there. There was just one solitary figure. A small boy about the same age as Susie, idly scooping items out of the water. When questioned this boy had no knowledge of her offspring; he'd only just come to the pools, and no one was there when he had arrived.

Her head in a spin she ran in the opposite direction, calling their names in a frenzy. People began to look at her strangely and one or two came forward to help. It was useless. No one had spotted them, though one woman remembered seeing Helen arriving at the beach with her children at the beach two or three hours before. She began to weep, softly at first, then the tears began to pour down her cheeks. She felt paralysed with fear, so numb that she felt she could not move. Actually, she always believed that she passed out for a few seconds. She distinctly remembered coming round with someone fanning her face and saying, "It's alright love. Come on have a sip of water". By now at least 90 minutes had passed since the children had left on their fishing expedition. Where could they be? Horrible thoughts flashed through her tormented mind. TV images flashed into her brain. Stories of tortured and maimed children. Children murdered. Children never found. And all the while those screeching seagulls overhead, mocking her in her distress.

"I think you should contact the police," a stocky middle-aged woman said gently.

This provoked another bout of sobs from her, but she tried to gather herself together, and galvanise herself into some kind of action. Not for the first time she rued the fact that she was a single parent. No-one to share this agony with; no one to hold her hand and support her in this torment.

She made the agonising walk back to the car, and drove into town to the local police station, which mercifully was easy to find. Mindful of her tear-streaked face, she poked furiously at it with a grubby tissue, trying to wash away the tracks of her tears. She entered the police station to find a young officer who looked about 12 on the desk.

"I've lost my children," she blurted out.

"How long ago," came the stock reply.

"About three hours now. They must have got lost on the beach."

"Easily done," came the unconcerned answer. "I'll just go and get a recording sheet".

Frustrated by the lack of urgency Helen felt the tears prickling at the back of her eyes again. She had to use all her resolve to stop the fountain behind her eyes cascading again.

There seemed an inordinately long wait before the young officer returned, accompanied by a much more mature officer with a twinkle in his eye and portly belly. "Lost two young children, eh?

Wouldn't be a boy of about four and a little girl of six, would it?"

Helen's heart lurched. "Well, yes. Do you know where they are?"

"Know where they are love? They are round the back eating ice cream."

Helen nearly fainted with relief. "Are you sure?" she quizzed.

"Take a look for yourself and see."

She was led into a small, but light, airy and room and there, sitting on the floor was Toby grinning from ear to ear, chocolate ice cream smeared all over his face, completely unabashed. "We've had a great time mum".

He looked so tiny in his miniscule red swimming trunks, she had to bite back her tears. Susie, looking slightly worried, with the wisdom of her extra two years, ran up and cuddled her mother. "I knew you'd come mum."

The now weeping Helen held her precious children to her heart. As they left the station, she could hear the seagulls shrieking on the shoreline. The sound would haunt her forever.

~~~

# In the Public Eye
## Hazel Burgess

She sashayed into the elegant Mayfair hotel. Her hips swung sensuously and her spiky heels clicked on the marble floor. Sitting in the plush lounge, on either side of a table littered with large cups of foaming, milky coffee and plates of enticing, sticky, jam-decorated pastries, were two young men, like book ends in their identical, widely striped navy-blue suits, crisp white shirts and bright silky ties. She took a seat confidently, sinking into the velvety easy chair, smoothing down her tight black skirt, placing her bright pink briefcase on the floor next to her and crossing her slender legs encased in sheer black nylon.

"So, Geraldine, you are going to present our new daytime magazine show," said one of the two men.

Geraldine discreetly extracted some sheets of paper from her briefcase, cleared her throat and started to run through her ideas for a show full of glitz, glamour and celebrities. She became increasingly passionate, remembering her previous show when she had been lucky enough to interview an up-and-coming pop star, winner of the reality show, Pop Champion and climbing to number 1 in the charts. This had been the making of her television career, soaring in the TV ratings and becoming a familiar figure in everyone's home. Her sleek, black bob, long, glossy pink finger nails and dangling earrings were as well recognised as the pop star; she was known for her hard, direct, challenging approach, succeeding in a man's world of early mornings in the studio, business lunches and late nights in the local Wine Bar. No-one dared cross her – they knew her research was thorough, digging out small pieces of detail submerged in their past and asking questions cunningly, expanding on their personal revelations, leaving her in glory and them in danger of a rapid fall down. No member of the paparazzi had yet found her weak spot, or discovered that enticingly embarrassing photograph. She was the Queen of daytime TV and the essence of success emanated from her glamorous personage in that hotel lounge.

The two men, career-minded individuals on a competitive ladder, climbing upwards, had the confidence of youth. They trusted

Geraldine and knew her success would mean their success also. They listened to her ideas, falling over themselves to offer to source material and to contact celebrity agents, finding the best and most dazzling guests for the show. Geraldine nibbled on a sticky cake and sipped her coffee gratefully, she had experienced a busy morning although it was only 10 o'clock. She nodded from time to time, and smiled her famous smile. This was going to work, another success story was practically in the bag. The show would be broadcast three days a week, she would have a team working behind the scenes and she would be the front person, resplendent on the renowned bright pink couch, with her glass of champagne, quizzing the rich and famous on the intricacies of their lives, the humdrum and the glitz.

With a shake of hands, the meeting closed. The two young entrepreneurs sank with relief back into the easy chairs and ordered large pints of beer to enjoy with their luxury chip butties.

Gerry let out a deep breath as she left the hotel, slipping down the dustbin strewn alleyway at the side of the building. Gratefully she slipped off the shiny patent high heels and took a pair of trainers and beige mac out of her capacious, and now empty, briefcase. With a sigh, she noticed the ladder creeping up from the toe of her sheer stockings. She breathed in, tensing her stomach muscles – the skirt felt so tight and she should be cutting down on sweet, sugary comfort food and full-fat milky drinks. She brushed her hand over the shoulders of her dark jacket, hoping her dry hair had not left tell-tale signs of dandruff – her nail started to come away, where the glue had failed to secure it properly. Oh dear, was that a breakfast stain on her lapel?

It was going to be hard to get back into the world of work. Gerry had to remember that she was now a 'working Mum'. With a pang she remembered the sweet-smelling, gum-less, grinning, baby boy she had left this morning, after he had spat his breakfast onto her best jacket and pulled at the shiny earrings. She flipped open her phone to speed-dial Tom, husband and daddy and that famous pop star she had interviewed three years earlier. She vanished incognito into the crowd, head down, talking into her phone, like all the other anonymous women trying to maintain a seamless working and home life.

~~~

# The Cellar
## Jackie Rickard

Tom was unusually nervous. He had decided he needed to get on the property ladder and find a suitable fair priced house to call his own. Although he and Sarah had been dating for quite a while, he still was not sure about their future together or otherwise.

Tom was a bit of a ditherer where decisions were concerned and was still happily living with his parents in their comfortable 3 up 2 down semi just outside Cardiff. His older brother had joined the Navy and came home as regularly as he was able but Tom was a little reluctant to leave the comfort and security of the family home to venture out on his own with no real reason to move other than it seemed the right thing to do and stand on his own two feet.

House prices were well within his means and he had a fairly secure job at the local building supplies which was handy he thought for when it came to renovating a property, he could get a sizeable staff discount on fittings and home improvements. But today might be the day for his whole world to change!! The local Auctioneers were holding an open sale day and he had spotted in their catalogue quite a nice cottage just up the road from his parent's house, perhaps not too far away but the first step to that home ownership, after all he was 38 and perhaps the time was right.

Oh Dad, would you come with me today, you're more experienced than I am and it is a big decision. His father readily agreed and off the two men went in search of bricks and mortar.

Eventually after what seemed an eternity, the small end terrace cottage came up for auction; 40,000... 42,000... 45,000... Tom held his nerve and eventually there seemed to be himself and one other person bidding. Eventually at £52,500 the hammer went down and in a blur of emotion Tom found himself, paddle in hand displaying his auction number, purchasing the cottage he had set out that morning to buy.

After a few days whilst money was exchanged, Tom collected the keys to his first property and gradually moved some possessions into his new house. There seemed more improvements than at first appeared and looking around the task seemed formidable, but he had acquired an inner strength and purpose for this exciting project. Everything needed improving as the cottage had not been lived in for about four years. The previous owners had been a bit of a mystery and had hardly been seen but that did not bother Tom as he set about the task in hand. The loft space he could turn into a nice modern bath room and the lounge and dining room could be knocked into one larger living area. Upon exploration what he originally thought of as a store cupboard next to the old-fashioned black range led to a small flight of stairs down to a pokey, dingy cellar. Now this had not appeared in the catalogue description, only the fact that everything was a little tired and there was room for improvement to the property.

Builders and decorators came and went quite rapidly for the more urgent improvements, then Tom decided it was time to do something with the old cellar, perhaps a games room with a snooker table and drinks bar where he and friends could enjoy some relaxation time. The cellar could soon be enlarged by knocking out a small wall then there would be ample space for a full-size snooker table if he could afford it. The wall was not load bearing for the main structure of the cottage so Tom and his dad set about demolishing it with sledge hammers and drills. It did seem odd that the wall appeared to be hollow once the first sledge hammer had been wielded and it was an easier task taking out the bricks than at first had been thought.

Once the initial dust and debris had settled the men could see an old leather Doctors type bag settled in one corner, Tom climbed his way over and dragging it to the light opened it to reveal it stashed with £20- and £50-pound notes. They lifted out rolls and rolls of dusty, dirty bank notes but all still legal tender.

So many thoughts went through their heads as to how the money had got there, why was it buried in a wall in a cellar, whose was it, who knew it was there and more importantly who should they tell about their find. Or should they not tell anyone!!

They sat on the floor surrounded by dust and debris all night pondering their next move. Neither of them had ever seen that amount of money before let alone touched it or counted it. They knew the right thing to do was to hand it into the local Police Station and be honest about their find and let the authorities unravel the mystery.

And unravel the mystery they eventually did. It would seem there had been a robbery four years earlier from a bank vault in Cardiff, the police had eventually rounded up the gang but the stolen money was never found. The three-man gang had holed up in the quiet little end terraced house before splitting and making their getaway fully intending to return to the cottage when it was safe to do so and collect their haul. Unfortunately for them they had been apprehended, tried and jailed and the case had been closed.

The money was eventually returned to its rightful place in the bank with a sizeable reward to Tom, enough for him to fully refurbish that old cellar into a games room with a top of the range snooker table, spotlights and bar!!

~~~

# Flowers for Me Mam
## Bob Close

Me names Sarah Barrass an aa live in Bolden Colliery, County Durham, in the pit cottages, number 7 Jubilee Street. Mam says aa was born two years after the owld Queen died but that means nowt to me. Well anyhows aa'm eight year owld now an aa'd better tell ye aboot me family,

Aa nivver knew me Mam; she were dead and buried before me first birthday. Aa were four year owld when me Mam, well not me Mam, aa mean me Gran who aa thought was me Mam, towld me that me real Mam had died an that she were really me Gran. Aa didn't care. Me Gran was a lovely Mam and me Dad, well me Dad who was really me Granda, was alreet. Most o the time ee was doon the pit an if he wasn't there he'd be doon the club with his marrers, smokin' and drinkin' til the money or the time ran oot. Me real Dad, like me real Mam, had kicked the bucket years ago, well not that long ago but before aa was born. Died in a pit accident.

So aa was gannin haeme from school yesterday with me best friend Jess an we walked along by the burn then cut through the allotments. This gadgee was sitting in an owld chair chewin' baccy an admirin' his leek trench. Near the path there was a great big patch of bright yellow flowers.

Aa thought 'Me Mam would love those' so aa said

"Hey Mister, can aa hev some o' these flowers for me Mam?"

He laughed "Hinney ye can have the lot. Them's weeds."

Well aa took a great big clump and Jess took the rest. Aa left Jess at the end of Jubilee Stret and went up the lane and into oor backyard. Aa went past the netty an the coal house and into the scullery through the open backdoor. Me Mam was at the stove doin' wa tea (ye'd call it dinner) so didn't see me at first.

"Mam" aa said "Aave brought ye some flowers".

Mam stopped her stirrin and looked over. She didn't look pleased. She wasn't.

"Get those bliddy things oot o this hoose NOW!"

Mam doesn't get angry very often, only when aa've been

really naughty, an she nivver swears so aa knew summit was up. But aa didn't deserve this an aa burst into tears and ran oot and threw the flowers into the lane. When aa came back in Mam put her arms around me and gave me a big hug. "Sorry pet, that wasn't fair. Its aboot time aa told ye about ya Ma." We went into the kitchen (ye'd call it the living room) and she sat me down on the settee.

An this is what aa found oot. After aa was born me Mam did whatever she could to earn a crust like tatty pickin an that sort a thing. On the day she died she was on piece work for the farmer pullin up an cuttin' the tops and bottoms off swedes. Divvn't laugh; aa mean the turnip thingees not the people! Anyhow me poor Mam was usin' a curved cutter (ye'd call it a sickle) an she slipped in the clarts an fell on the blade. On the edge of the field it was, right next to patches of summat called Charlock; Yellow Charlock. Nowt they could do, poor Mam bled to death on the spot, her bright red blood spashing onter the bright yellow flowers. An them were the flowers aa'd brought haeme. Ne wonder me Mam was upset.

Aa started to say aa was sorry but me Mam gave me another hug and said "That's alreet pet, ye didn't mean any harm".

"What's gannin' on here?" said me Dad, standing in the doorway and wonderin'where is tea was.

Me Mam sighed gave me a pat on the head and went into the scullery to finish off her cookin'.

After a plate pie an mash we had rhubarb an custard for puddin. Aa love custard but divvn't much care for the rhubarb. Mam won't let me have one withoot the other so aa started to mix them up, stirrin the bright red rhubarb into the bright yellow custard.

"Hey Mam...'" aa started to say and then rhought I'd better not say what aa was thinkin'.

"What pet?" said me Mam.

"Smashin custard Mam" aa said an she looked dead pleased.

So now ye know, aa'm an orphan. But aa'm fine. Aa've got me Mam, whose me Gran, and she takes care of me. Aa couldn't have a better Mam….an me Dad, as aa said, is alreet. When aa grow up aa'm gonna be the best Mam, an the best Gran, in the whole world. Just like mine.

~~~

# Migration; The Bird on the Wire
## Bobby Cadwallader

I am old now. My mobility is somewhat restricted. My eyesight is poor. I do not think I can face another winter, however buoyant the breeze and fair the seas. It was not always so.

The day I saw the girl I was young, free and easy: light as a feather and hopelessly giddy with the intoxication of the atmosphere. There were thousands of us.

It was a day when humans don a jacket at 8am against the autumn chill but are almost invariably basking in their shirt sleeves by noon. On this day too, the rolling morning mist would evolve into glorious mellow September sunshine.

There she was with her impossible curls, straining under her homespun cap: her face smudged with tears, clutching a small duffel bag.

\*\*\*\*\*

I too am older. Not as old as I look, as the years have not been kind to me. The day I saw the bird I was finding it difficult to face the future. Seven years old and an orphan. Shivering in my thin gabardine, I pulled my knitted cap down further over my ears. It was too small for me now, knitted by my darling mum when I was only four. It was one of the few possessions I still had which clung to her memory. I stood on the quayside fearful, cold and very much alone.

\*\*\*\*\*

The girl caught my eye because she was so very tiny. Probably not the youngest or even the saddest. She looked the most lost. They all looked downcast, even the two boys kicking a deflated ball were performing half-heartedly. The group, of maybe a hundred children, made a forlorn picture, as they gathered by the water.

\*\*\*\*\*

On that day I was feeling bewildered, bemused, befuddled. My short life had descended rapidly into chaos after my beloved mum had died. Plunged into the anonymity of the local orphanage, after being cosseted in the warm loving life which my only known parent had created for me, was terrifying. Then, just as I was beginning to get used to the rigours and formality of institutional life, I had been ripped away again, and thrust unwillingly on to a boat. "Australia, land of hope and opportunity," they told us. It did not feel like it, nor did it prove to be so.

*****

The contrast of those pathetic, grimy children with our expectant and joyful congregation could not be greater. Our wings unfurling ready for flight, we were thrilled with the anticipation of clear skies, sparkling seas, warmer weather. Yes, these kids were about to sail these same seas, reach those warmer shores, but they would not be free like us. I looked down at this scrap of a girl and I wept for her.

*****

A woman pinned a label on my threadbare jacket. A label with my name and date of birth printed in a rough hand upon it. I felt like a parcel but certainly not a Christmas present. I looked shyly at the other children. Could I make any of them my friends? They all looked unkempt and a bit bedraggled. I knew too I was dishevelled but I certainly wasn't tough. Did any of them feel as bereft as I did? It was at that moment I saw the little bird on the wire. Perched slightly away from the others he was smaller but brighter. I could swear he was looking at me. I had heard of migration. My mum once told me about birds flying south for winter. On her sick bed she had romanced about flying south with them. "Oh, Annie if only I had wings to set me free." Maybe the warmer climate would have helped her recover. As I looked at my little bird singing his heart out, excited for the journey, and I watched his thousand companions preparing likewise, I thought of my mum and grieved for her. She never got to fly south. I was going in her place, but reluctantly, in trepidation and not in joyful flight like my little bird.

*****

As I sit on the wire, I perch a little away from my feathered friends. I know this will be my final flight. I recall that day so many years ago and ponder on my little girl. Today I appreciate her sentiments. A journey reluctantly taken. I know it will be my last and I shall end my days in warmer climes. I won't be coming back. I doubt that she did either.

~~~

# Freedom (to be safe and happy)
## Christine Campbell

I was sleeping when my mother came to tell me it was time. She was carrying the baby and with her free arm she helped me up then handed me the bundle I kept by me, ready for when we would leave.

My father picked up my blanket and holding it open enfolded me inside and carried me just as my baby brother was being cradled by my mother. In the same way, I held my doll Misha, in my arms. I was not frightened then, more curious to see where we were going and where we would end up.

For a long time, my mother had told me about a place where we would be safe and happy.I repeated the words over and over as I leaned against my father, gently being rocked by his steady footsteps.

It was dark but I could hear the sound of the waves and knew we were nearing the beach. I had seen the beach when we came here but we were not allowed to go away from the forest, so I tried to remember what the water looked like. There had seemed to be no end to it.

We left the road and my father's stride slowed. We were on the other side of the big mounds of sand that hid the beach from the road. Suddenly my father stopped and put me down on the sand. My mother came close and I held on to the side of her skirt. Father told us to come when he called, a low whistle like the sound of the owls in the nearby trees. My eyes had become accustomed to the blackness and I could see shapes moving near the water's edge, then came the call and we moved forward, my mother, brother and I and Misha.

The boat was small and I was squashed between my parents. There was a woman with a baby opposite and behind were two men who spoke to my father in a language I did not understand. We all knew to be silent.

The boat was rowed by the men for some while before a spluttering sound of an engine being started split the quiet of the night. My mother squeezed my shoulder and said it won't be long now.

I lay back and watched the moon lighting a path through the endless water. I must have fallen asleep because suddenly there was light all around and voices shouting. At first, I thought the moon had fallen into the boat but soon made out the shape of another much bigger boat nearby, with a great beam of light shining from it. My father was with the other men talking to the people on the big boat again in the language I did not understand. I asked my mother what was happening but she just said, "Don't worry, we will soon be safe and happy. These men are going to help us. Don't be scared".

I was lifted up and somehow placed into another pair of arms. I felt the wind on my face but the light was blinding. I seemed to be floating and then yet more arms, encircling me with a warm cloak. I pulled my hand free and saw that Misha was still in my grasp. The moon had disappeared and a glowing light was in the distance, the sun was coming up as it did every other day. "Look", I said to Mischa, "The sun is here, we will soon be safe and happy".

With the daylight came a new view, at the end of the water there were lights and different shapes of buildings. As we neared the land, I could see people waiting; my father was beside me and carried me from the boat through the shallow water towards the waiting people.

We sat inside a building with large windows, but there was nothing to see outside. My mother and baby brother were beside me and I asked what had happened to my father. He had been taken behind one of the many doors. Mother told me he would not be long; we were safe now. I felt safe but not happy.

Later we were all together and taken in a bus to another large building but this time there were trees outside and before I went inside, I heard birds singing. We were given something to eat but I can't remember what it was; I was so hungry that I just ate.

We stayed together in a room very high up in the building. There was a cot for my brother and a small bed for me, next to that of my parents. There was a television but we couldn't understand what the people were saying so my father tried to explain. He said soon you will go to school and you will learn how to speak this language.

We had been given new clothes, which I was pleased to have as this was a colder place than we were used to. I had shoes that covered my feet and felt strange but they helped me to run fast when we went outside to play. There were new toys for me and my brother, but I never played with the dolls as I didn't want to upset Misha. She even had a new dress and when we were tucked up in our bed at night, she told me that she felt safe and happy.

Now we live in a new house where there are many other houses. There are lots of children to play with; some of them speak the same language as me, but I am learning the language called English at my new school. My father goes to work in a big warehouse but he says he will carry on with his studies and I must do the same. He says we have been given a second chance and not everyone gets a second chance to be safe and happy.

~~~

# Just a Taste
## Hazel Burgess

Muriel had been coerced by her lady friends to dip her toe in the water. Tired of being an add-on, the spare woman, the lonely heart, she had signed up to the Find a Friend website – just a taste you understand. This was her first foray into the world of dating. Nervously she tweaked her hair over her ears, adjusted her lacy top and held the folded copy of The Times with its title prominently displayed.

Bill turned the corner, clutching his copy of the newspaper, and saw her standing outside the swanky hotel, with the fine dining restaurant recommended to him by his mother, who was desperate for him to fly the nest and become independent. This was his first taste of online matchmaking.

Sitting at the table, covered with a starched white cloth and gleaming silver, Bill was relieved he did not have to make any decisions. The menu was pre-determined and the wine came with it!

Muriel thought the man facing her looked rather nice – about her age, with light sandy hair and fair skin. He seemed to know what he was doing and smiled at her in a rather attractive way, crinkling his eyes and showing healthy white teeth.

She had never dined in a place like this before and was so pleased she did not have to choose from the array of exotic dishes.

*Amuse Bouche*
What was this? Was it supposed to be funny? The tiny morsel of crisp toast, topped with fish pate, crème fraiche and caviar seemed a very small starter. Bill had eaten it in one go and she giggled as he too looked perplexed.

Bill glanced at the menu and was relieved to see there was another course, which sounded like a starter.

*Smoked Salmon*
This was nothing like the smoked salmon that came in sandwiches at the local supermarket. Muriel gasped as two waiters

arrived bearing platters covered by a smoking dome. It looked like a crystal ball and she wondered if she would be able to forecast her future by staring into its swirling depths. Reflected in there she could see her and Bill, smiling in awe. The waiters whipped off the glass covers in synchronisation revealing the show piece appearing through the mist – a speciality of the house. The taste was out of this world – she could develop a passion for this.

*Turbot with Essence of Cauliflower*
The white fish looked resplendent on the black plate. Conversation had stalled as both she and Bill waited to see what the next treat would be. She hoped he was not a cold fish, that he had something interesting to talk about and would turn out to be as affectionate as his profile had hinted.

Bill stared open mouthed at tiny sliced char-grilled florets of cauliflower, cauliflower puree and what looked like a cauliflower bhaji, although nothing like the one from the local take away. He thought of the beautiful, fresh produce he had helped his grandfather grow on his allotment and started to talk to Muriel about his love of the outdoors and sustainable living.

Wow – a man after her own heart. Muriel listened with enthusiasm and told him how she loved crafting home-baked bread and trying new recipes. She thought she might get some ideas tonight.

By this time the white wine stopped flowing to be replaced by a robust red which seemed to reflect in the glow from her cheeks. She really was rather attractive thought Bill.

*Sorbet*
This small blob of champagne flavoured ice was not the dessert, was it? Bill worried she would think him a penny pincher, as his stomach rumbled and he spooned it in. The menu said it was a palate cleanser. Muriel had no idea what that was either, but thought it could not be anything like toothpaste or mouth wash! They looked at each other and chuckled.

*Filet of Beef*

Steak and chips it was not! Muriel thought the tender meat, nicely pink, garnished with foie gras, slivers of bone marrow, delicately carved carrots and parsnips, pommes puree (not mash) and a rich red wine jus was sublime. Bill felt the red blood flowing through his veins, giving him confidence to compliment his companion, to look her in the eye and to let his gaze drop to the décolleté neckline of her pretty blouse. Flushed, Muriel simpered up at him, fluttering her eyelashes whilst delicately dabbing the corners of her mouth. She felt quite giddy, not alcohol induced but a fluttering she had never experienced before.

*Pre Dessert*

The porcelain spoon, rather like those in the Chinese restaurant, proudly carried a round of light chocolate mousse, decorated with a strawberry. They were getting used to this menu of different tastes by now and Bill watched as her tongue shot out and licked slowly around the edge. He felt his tongue doing the same thing and reddened as he thought of them doing it together. Without knowing how, he found his hand had crept across the table and his fingers were touching the tips of her newly lacquered pink nails.

Muriel liked the feeling of his fingers against hers and started to let her hand creep nearer as the next course arrived.

*Pear with Honey*

The plate was adorned with a golden sugar pear. They tapped the crisp shell with their spoons, in harmony. Would the magic of the evening shatter with the shards of sugar, leaving hearts broken into many pieces? Would dreams come crashing down? Was this the end before it had begun? Inside was a soft heart, a sweet honey mousse, melting in the mouth. Muriel's friends had always told her she had a heart of gold. She smiled softly – Bill was already finding his way to her soft heart. Likewise, Bill felt his heart melting as he gazed at the beautiful woman of his dreams.

*Cheese*

The fortified wine brought new courage. The robust flavours

of stilton and cheddar, the creaminess of brie rounded off a perfect meal. Bill felt he could slay dragons, rescue a damsel in distress, gallop into the night with Muriel in his arms. He felt assured and confident. Muriel willed him to save her from her lonely life.

*Coffee*
With the perfectly ground, mellow coffee came small squares of icing-sugar encrusted Turkish Delight. Bill gazed at his very own Turkish Delight, licking the white powder from her lips. She had her own, sweet soft centre and he would find out more. Muriel gazed at her knight in shining armour, thinking how worldly he was, how he had taken such care of her tonight and what a wonderful companion he was.

Together they left the restaurant and walked into the moonlit streets, heads bowed, talking softly and anticipating the future together. This had been just a taste of something better to come.

~~~

# A Fresh Start
## Jackie Rickard

'Oh My Goodness' thought Cindy as she sat on the stony terrace, glass of red wine in hand, reflecting on the day and taking in the magnificent views across the valley in front of her, with the sandy, gravel ground and the enormous green trees and in the far distance the red and orange of the setting sun.

'Paradise doesn't come much better than this'. She could hear Pasqual coming to join her, his sandals crunching down on the gravel terrace as he approached and gently, so very gently, putting his hand on her shoulder, bent down to give her a warm and loving kiss. He sat beside her, wine glass in one hand and holding her close. Neither spoke as they enjoyed the wine and watched the setting sun together.

Their different worlds had only come together by accident a few months earlier when Cindy had been hurriedly leaving a coffee shop, takeaway skinny latte in one hand and an armful of paperwork in the other when she literally bumped into this stranger, managing to hold tightly onto the coffee but the paperwork scattering over the pavement. They both instinctively bent down to retrieve the papers, before looking into each other's eyes and at that very moment they both knew something special had just happened. His warm, romantic eyes seemed to devour her completely, that along with his tan and shoulder length wavy hair captivated her.

Cindy was a lawyer on her way to Court to defend a petty thief, not one of her most interesting of cases and Pasqual was enjoying his last few days in London before moving to France. He had been roving around Italy, Spain and France mending a broken ego after his fiancée had decided to call time on their romance. Or was it a broken heart? He could not really decide if it was for the best that him and Natalie had parted at her request, or should he have been the one to approach the subject. After all they had been drifting apart and becoming more like friends than lovers for a few months now, both in a comfort zone neither had the courage to leave.

He had been in London to sign for the completion on the purchase of a Chateau in France, one he had spotted when he took a wrong turning along the country roads near the Loire Valley. He had stopped his car and fallen in love instantly with the run-down building in front of him. Okay it needed a bit of work, well a lot of work really if he had been honest with himself, but he knew it had the possibility to be the most fabulous Chateau in the whole world. His laid-back romantic outlook to life had convinced him a bit of rendering on the outside and some painting on the inside would easily spruce up this building. He could picture in his mind the opulent staircases and ornate high ceilings were the perfect setting for his new venture, with outbuildings ripe for conversion into a Wedding and Celebration venue complete with lake and horse-riding facilities.

On retrieving all Cindy's paperwork and the exchanging of 'phone numbers, there they were that evening sat in a quiet corner of a local restaurant, talking, laughing, planning. She recalled later that she had not been that relaxed and happy for many months.

Her colleagues were dumfounded, almost speechless and slightly bemused when she informed them the next day of her intentions to quit her job and start afresh with Pasqual and his dream of a Wedding Venue Chateau in France.

Well today had been moving in day, no turning back now! Ahead lay hard, rewarding work transforming this run-down ruin into a Palace and their forever home. Friends had promised to visit and the venue hire diary had bookings already.

What more could they both wish for, a fresh start for both of them.

~~~

# A Curious Incident
Bob Close

In 1966 four of us drove a customised Bedford Dormobile a total of 11,000 miles around the Mediterranean as something different to do on our Summer Break from university. Part of this Grand Tour took us across the vast expanse of the North Libyan desert. As we crossed the border from Tunisia we looked forward to panoramic views of the endless sands of the Sahara; such imaginings being occasioned by a recent viewing of 'Lawrence of Arabia'.

At the time we were not aware that the Sahara is not actually *in* Arabia. Our ignorance was perhaps forgivable since none of us were studying geography and we were also singularly lacking in general knowledge and indeed common sense. We were students; need I say more. However, the expectation of a sandy landscape in North Africa was perhaps not entirely ridiculous, even for students.

Unfortunately, the Libyan reality was mile after mile of rocky scrubland, a wasteland of rubble and unforgiving, thorned flora. After 300 miles of mainly dead straight road through this desolation, and as night fell, we looked in vain for a patch of rock-free ground on which to sleep. Miraculously we found one and pulled off to the side of the road. After a rushed supper of cold baked beans, straight from the tin, we collapsed into our sleeping bags and crashed out.

We slept the silent, dark, sleep of the dead until an urgent voice fractured the silence, a light punctured the blackness, and in an instant we were awake.

An old Arab man stood above us, lantern in hand. He smiled encouragingly, spoke rapidly, earnestly, and to us incomprehensibly, but clearly indicated, through frantic gestures, that we should get up and follow him. Grumbling and cursing we awkwardly dressed inside our sleeping bags then stumbled after him along a narrow trail. Finally, we arrived at a tiny hut of corrugated iron and he indicated that we should enter. Inside the hut we sat on a dry, dusty floor as the old man brewed mint tea on a small wood stove. Small glasses of the sweet, pungent brew were passed to us and as we sipped at our drinks, he excitedly brought out from a corner of the hut a small wooden box. He lifted the lid and carefully extracted flimsy sheets with apparent illustrations on them. We were each given a single sheet and as he passed them over, he said, slowly and carefully "Christian". And again "Christian".

We looked at the sheets and on each of them there were four biblical images – The wedding at Cana, Abraham and Isaac, Ruth gleaning the fields, David and Goliath. They were religious stickers, the kind I had been given every week as an infant at Sunday School, one a week in the expectation that we would ultimately complete an album we were also given. "Christian" the old man emphasised and then beamed as we nodded in affirmation. We pointed at him and said "Christian?". He smiled and shook his head, "Muslim" he said softly "Muslim". He beamed at us as we finished our tea and then indicated that he would take us back to our van.

We offered back the sheets but he vigorously refused to take them. It was clear they were a gift. Where had he got them from and for how long he had waited for the opportunity to pass them on we did not know and could not find out. Clearly this moment held considerable meaning for him.

We bowed our thanks to our benefactor and he finally led us back to our temporary camp site.

We attempted to give him something in return but he made it clear that he would take nothing.

"Barakah Allah" (may Allah bless you) he said solemnly to each of us and then he turned and wandered back up the trail to his home.

Later as I lay contemplating the heavens and reflecting on the kindness of strangers it occurred to me that, although 'The wedding at Cana' and 'David and Goliath' were welcome additions to my sticker collection I still needed 'Moses at the Midianite well' to complete the album.

~~~

# The Way to be Free; The Bird on the Wire
## Christine Campbell

The whole world stretches out before me, little parcels of green and blocks of orange. It looks familiar but strange, I haven't been this high before.

Once I was part of that world, the one below; now I can soar above or swoop down to be part of it again but not as I used to be.

I remember the garden; I used to tend it most days. It became more difficult over time when I could no longer bend to remove the weeds or trim the lower branches. I remember the herb bed; the smell of the lavender, rosemary and marjoram were comforting to me, as I rubbed the leaves between the papery skin of my fingers and breathed deeply. Memories of sun-baked Mediterranean villages invaded my senses and once more my body felt pain free, smooth and supple.

Now the sun has gone. I sleep most of the day; sometimes I wake when it is dark, sometimes it is the light that wakes me.

I am playing a waiting game; I know my time is near and I wait in anticipation.

Last night, or it may have been the morning, I sensed someone in the room near me. I didn't see them, but felt a presence, a comforting warmth. This entity stroked my forehead, told me all would be well and to prepare for my journey.

I watched the swallows from my window each evening, dipping and diving, their cries calling to me. Oh to be free, to feel the warm air lift me and release me from the constraints of this room, this bed, this pain.

\*\*\*\*\*

If you could be any animal what would you be? This was a game we used to play with the children on long journeys. As we made our way from the ferry port through the motorways and cypress lined roads of the south of France, we explored the options. James always favoured something fierce, like a lion, tiger or bear and tried out the various noises, not sure of the difference between a lion and a tiger so deciding a bear would be preferable, but not a polar bear as he didn't like the cold. Annabel was always a cat, soft and gentle with a plaintive miaow. My husband would be an eagle, soaring high and looking down on the world; quite apt in the circumstances, he being a distinguished professor and expert in his field.

And me - I was always the swallow; the bird on the wire, with its soothing, twittering song and its loop-the-loop flight, it is a welcome sight in our skies every spring. I listened to my children's cries of "mummy's always a swallow", then collapsing in laughter as they made loud gulping noises to illustrate them swallowing.

My mind would wander as I recalled the Leonard Cohen song, part of the soundtrack to those heady, languid days passing slowly in that long hot summer of 69; bare feet, long floaty dresses, beads round our necks and a feeling that anything was possible.

"Like a bird on the wire / like a drunk in a midnight choir / I have tried in my way to be free."

I took the path of the swallow, in reverse, that summer; our battered VW camper van resting its weary joints as we made our way across the channel, then stirring into life to putter down the empty roads of western France, stopping to buy bread, cheese and wine in achingly beautiful villages clinging on to the rocky hillsides; evenings spent under the stars with others like us, who craved freedom and change, not realising the two were mutually exclusive. We meandered on through Spain, losing some of our companions on the way but collecting others like a ragged procession of sleepwalkers all following the pied piper of their dreams.

Autumn found us in Morocco - pioneers of the hippie trail to Marrakech then on to the coast where we found our Shangri-La in Essaouira, a haven for inspiration, a place to rest and work out just what the hell we had been doing for the last nine months.

When the swallows returned heading to their winter resting place with their new families, we remained with our new family of kindred spirits; the poets, the musicians, thinkers and dreamers, and gently tried to change the world with words, music and beautiful thoughts.

We never quite made it, and as the sixties merged into the seventies we caved in and returned, back to London, to nine to five office jobs, a two up two down terraced house and plans to start a family.

But every spring I waited like a mother welcoming her children home from a gap year as my feathered friends took up their summer board in the eaves of the barn.

The swallows are waiting for me. When summer ends, look up and you'll see me – a bird on the wire.

~~~

# Autumn Days
## Bobby Cadwallader

She had always loved the Autumn; the glorious colours of the leaves as they fell to earth like a golden shower of rain; the crunchy sound underfoot as she took those precious Sunday morning walks; the glistening blackberries that stained her fingers as she plucked them to cram into her mouth; the always unexpected beauty of the first sight of the burnished conkers as she peeled them from their prickly shells and, that marvellous uplifting Autumn song which echoed her thoughts and reflected her emotions so accurately. "The jewelled grass and the jet planes meeting in the air" filled her heart with gladness and anticipation as the children bellowed out the words in assembly.

She had always regarded Autumn as a new beginning. The start of a new year. The blank page and the newly sharpened pencils which held such promise. She always loved returning to school as a child, seeing her friends again after the long summer break and getting back into the academic world. She loved school and studying. Then as a teacher greeting a whole new group of fresh faced and mostly eager students in her painstakingly displayed classroom. The utter joy she experienced in acquainting herself with these new little personalities and the excitement at recognising their potential and being part of their future development always gave her such a thrill.

In addition to all of this her birthday was in October. She adored birthdays even as an adult and always made sure that something exciting was arranged. Frequently she spent the weekend in a foreign city though more recently she had been entertained by her grandchildren with their home-made cards and messages of love to the moon and back.

This year it was different. The Autumn Pageant was as splendid as ever. The trees were a riot of colour. The chestnuts were still hiding in their hedgehog shells and the blackberries were just as plentiful and juicier than ever. Moreover, she no longer needed to restrict her walks to Sunday mornings. But even then, when she had ventured out on a crisp, sparkling Monday morning, across mist covered fields to the next village she had been suddenly overwhelmed with sadness at the sight of an old sign at the back of the church yard heralding "Cream teas every Sunday". The peeling paint and dilapidated state of the hoarding made her feel miserable and forsaken.

After this discovery, although she could not deny the majesty of the world in which she walked, she felt downcast and depressed. Her birthday plans were in full swing. She was heading to her beloved Norfolk and she could extend her weekend to four or five days now that she was a free agent. But somehow that very word free made her shudder. Maybe the fact that she had fallen and injured herself for the second time in as many months had something to do with her mood. She was certainly unhappy that her exercise routine had been severely restricted owing first to her sprained ankle and now bruised ribs. She could feel herself putting on weight and feeling uncharacteristically lethargic. Perhaps she was also feeling her age. This had not been helped by a call from the doctor's surgery, a place she almost never went, to tell her she was now eligible for a flu jab. Reluctantly she had presented herself for the indignity of the needle. She regretted the fact that she had not taken herself off somewhere exotic on 3rd September when the children returned to school. Her mood had not been helped by the fact she lived in a cul de sac with a primary school at its head. On the first day of term, she heard the eager voices and saw the crisp new uniforms, polished shoes and the shining morning faces of the children who, rather than "creeping like snails unwillingly to school" were rushing headlong excitedly into a new year. She was reminded of Jacques' speech in "As you like it". If there were seven ages of man then she had to be in the sixth. She did not like the sound of "the lean and slipper'd pantaloons" even though she did now have "spectacles on nose". She recognised in herself a reluctance to admit to ageing.

But of course, retirement heralded old age. No one could escape this reality. She began to reflect on why she was feeling so untethered and out of sorts. Her life until now had always had such purpose, such routine. On her retirement she had looked forward to flexibility, variety, spontaneity and definitely no responsibility. How had she got it so horribly wrong? Reflecting again on Shakespeare's words she dismissed the sixth age and reminded herself that she was actually only in the Autumn of her life preferred to feel she was in the autumn of her life, and Autumn, she had always told herself, was full of promise. She must reinvent herself somehow. As she heard the all too familiar sound of the bell summoning the students to their studies she realised that what she missed was not the routine, not the organisation, but the children themselves. It came to her in a flash. She could volunteer to help in school. Reading, washing the paint pots, mounting displays... anything. That way she would reconnect with the children but have none of the responsibility. She could regain the buzz that the children always afforded her. It was a start. After that she would think about joining some other organisations where she might develop some different talents. She reached for the phone and dialled the number of the school.

~~~

# Flying High; The Bird on the Wire
Hazel Burgess

This was what he had come for; he had been waiting for this moment. He held his breath and gazed upwards, watching in anticipation.

The smell of new mown grass assailed his nostrils; the fuggy atmosphere and heat enveloped him. Harry exhaled slowly as she stepped out on to the wire. A bright flash of turquoise reflected against the dirty cream background. She trembled as a cautious foot stepped out, felt its footing, then she arched her back with confidence and spread her arms wide.

The artiste reminded Harry of a bird, caught in the lofty chamber of the Big Top. He had been visiting every day for a week now, he who had never been to a circus as a boy. His first visit had been out of curiosity. With time to kill he had found himself walking past the annual circus on the Recreation Ground. Peering through the fencing he had advanced towards the ticket booth where, trapped in the ubiquitous queue of eager spectators, weary looking mothers, frazzled fathers and screaming, excited children, he had really had no choice but to hand over his pensioner's 5 pounds. Taking a rickety chair on the back row he had prepared to see what he always wondered happened in the cavernous tent.

The lions, elephants and clowns were much as expected from the information he had gleaned as a boy from comic books and idle gossip in the playground. Then the top of the bill, 'The Little Bird', had stepped out on to the wire. Mesmerised, he had watched as she gained her balance and stepped out on to the wire, one foot at a time. Her confidence amazed him; it was magical to watch. A slight, slender girl, in her leotard of bright blue/green, pale pink tights and ballet slippers to match, a dark ponytail tied back in its ribbon. The audience had gasped as she made her way across the tent, sometime wobbling slightly as she poised, one foot in the air, before taking the next step. As she neared the other side a young man in black swung a trapeze in her direction. So, she descended a little, somersaulting on the bar, swinging with two arms, then one, like a bird taking off.

As she soared back up, abandoning the trapeze for a curtain

call on the wire, she seemed to bow straight in Harry's direction. He vowed he must come and see her again. He did, every day for the past week, each day sitting further forward to get closer.

Today was the last day the circus was in town. Harry had researched its itinerary to see if he might follow it to its next destination but it appeared this was its last venue. He did not want the bird to go; she reminded him of his wife, Maggie, as a young girl. Dark and pretty, dancing round the ballroom as free as a bird, she had captured his heart and had done so for fifty years. How he missed her, the tinkling laughter, the bravery when she said, 'Come on, Harry, give it a go.' Oh, she had made him brave and, because of her influence, he had travelled the world, seen the sights, done what tourists do. Flying high in a hot air balloon, skimming down a hillside in a straw toboggan, teetering on chairlifts, hanging suspended in a cable car, travelling at supersonic speed in Concorde. Yet he had always hated heights but could not bring himself to disappoint Maggie. She would have loved to walk a high wire and swing from a trapeze.

On that day six months ago, he had consoled himself by imagining her soul flying high, up to heaven. He knew how she would want to go and had sent her ashes up in a rocket, way into the heavens then floating down to the expansive moorland he had chosen as her favourite destination. A few friends had come, but there were no children; it had never happened and as the years had rolled by the opportunity was lost.

So now he was alone, with only his dreams. Shambling out of the field he decided the Little Bird could have been Maggie's daughter; how she would have loved to watch her. Fingering his bus pass, he decided it was time to take a trip out of town.

Behind the scenes in the Big Top Margrit wiped the grease paint from her rubbery skin, tired from the daily application, and weather beaten from outdoor living. She was getting too old for this. The faded leotard bagged around her body, over stretched from so much wear. Her tights wrinkled around her ankles, snagged from her daily adventures on the wire. It had almost been a close call today. Sergio had not put enough chalk on her shoe and she had thought she was going to fall, feeling the clasp of the safety wire and looking beneath her to make sure the net was there. It was time for their annual vacation, back to Romania, where she could reunite with her two growing boys in the care of her elderly parents. They had no aspirations to join the circus but it provided the income for their ongoing education and treats, something Margrit and Sergio had never had.

For a brief moment she had made the mistake of looking down today, head swimming. She had seen the old man gazing up at her from the front row. Tears had come to her eyes as she thought of her father, patiently waiting for her annual visit to see him. 'Time to pack up and go,' Sergio, the love of her life, strode towards her, smiling brightly. Next year would be their last, she determined. It was time to go home.

Dismounting from the country bus Harry strode across the moor, gazing upwards to see the birds soaring higher and higher, close to Maggie. One day soon he would join her, never mind that he would have to fly.

~~~

## About the authors

### Jackie Rickard

Jackie was a highly enthusiastic member of our group. A former school secretary, she joined to, 'keep her brain challenged.' She produced some very amusing stories, particularly about her family. She was the centre of that close-knit and happy family and is greatly missed by us all.

### Bob Close

Now retired, Bob Close is a former lecturer in Biology. On leaving the world of teaching he worked for the charity *War Child* as a senior administrator and for a short time as stand-in CEO. He was a founding member of the charity *Garden Africa* and has also worked for a small company specialising in the creation of educational books for children. His work experiences have convinced him that truth is indeed stranger than fiction.

### Christine Campbell

Chris retired from the NHS after 15 years, during lockdown, when she got used to having time to explore other pursuits, including brushing up her writing skills. She says she is a frustrated journalist but now enjoys writing for pleasure. She belongs to several U3A groups, two choirs, and is secretary of a local Scottish Country Dancing club. She is a grandmother, and has just welcomed a new grandson for whom she will write some stories.

## Bobby Cadwallader

Bobby is a retired head teacher, now a yoga fanatic and a keen traveller. She is always trying to emulate her glorious mother who is a Bletchley Park veteran and, at 102, is still her role model. She is also a mother, a grandmother, an enthusiastic baker, a vigorous walker and of course, sometimes, a writer.

## Hazel Burgess

Hazel has been a member of Aylesbury U3A for eleven years and was a founder member of its first Creative Writing Group. As someone who enjoys 'people watching' she relishes the opportunity to sneak these observations into her writing.